Daniel Plays at School

adapted by Daphne Pendergrass
based on the screenplay "Problem Solver Daniel"
written by Becky Friedman
poses and layouts by Jason Fruchter

Ready-to-Read

Simon Spotlight
New York London Toronto Sydney New Delhi

SIMON SPOTLIGHT
An imprint of Simon & Schuster Children's Publishing Division
1230 Avenue of the Americas, New York, New York 10020
This Simon Spotlight edition September 2020

For information about special discounts for bulk purchases, please contact Simon & Schuster Special Sales at 1-866-506-1949 or business@simonandschuster.com.
Manufactured in the United States of America 0920 LAK
2 4 6 8 10 9 7 5 3 1
ISBN 978-1-4814-6104-7 (eBook)
ISBN 978-1-5344-4331-0 (prop)

Hi, neighbor!
Welcome to my school.

“Do you want to play?”
asks Miss Elaina.

Yes!

I want to build a train.
Miss Elaina wants
to build a spaceship.

We want to build
different things.

"What should we do?"
We ask Teacher Harriet.

She says, “Try to solve the problem yourself. You will feel proud.”

We talk about
our problem.
We have an idea!

We will build
a space train!

This block is
the engine.

These are
the rockets.

And these blocks are the wings!

We did it!

“How do you feel?”
Teacher Harriet asks.

We feel proud!

It is time for our
space train to blast off!

Prince Wednesday
wants to play with us!

Miss Elaina will drive the train.

W

I will be a space alien.
I will wear this
green jacket!

Prince Wednesday
wants to be a
space alien too.

We both want to wear
the jacket.
What should we do?

Try to solve the
problem yourself.
You will feel proud.

We have an idea!
We can both wear
the jacket!

We are a silly
space alien together.

Now we can blast off
to space school!

I liked solving problems
at school today.
Ugga Mugga!